VOLUME
9

Story: Darren Shan
Manga: Takahiro Arai

THE SAGA OF
DARREN SHAN
THE VAMPIRE PRINCE

A SUMMARY OF TRIALS OF DEATH:

FACING ALMOST CERTAIN DEATH FOR FAIL-
ING THE TRIALS OF INITIATION, DARREN
CONSPIRES WITH KURDA AND GAVNER
TO ESCAPE FROM VAMPIRE MOUNTAIN.
BUT ALONG THE ESCAPE ROUTE, KURDA'S
TRUE ALLIANCE WITH THE VAMPANEZE
BECOMES APPARENT, AND GAVNER IS
KILLED. HIS BEST RESISTANCE PROVEN
FUTILE, CORNERED BY THE VAMPANEZE,
DARREN'S ONLY ESCAPE IS THROUGH THE
MOUNTAIN'S GIANT AQUEDUCT. SPURN-
ING KURDA'S HAND OF RESCUE, DARREN
THROWS HIMSELF INTO THE SWIRLING
MAELSTROM THAT CARRIES HIM AWAY
FROM VAMPIRE MOUNTAIN...

THE VAMPIRE PRINCE
CONTENTS

...MAY I BE TRIUMPHANT!!!

EVEN IN DEATH...

CHAPTER 45: RAPIDS

...AND SURRENDERED MYSELF TO THE VICIOUS FLOW OF THE STREAM.

I IGNORED KURDA'S HELPING HAND...

GOON (KFWOOOSH)

...SWIFTLY SWEPT UNDERGROUND, INTO THE BELLY OF VAMPIRE MOUNTAIN.

AND I HEADED INTO DARKNESS, INTO CERTAIN DEATH...

CHAPTER 45:
RAPIDS

STRANGE-LY, THERE WAS NO PAIN, NO FEAR...

BOGI
(GRNCH)

BAGU
(GRAKK)

...SHARP EDGES CUTTING ME DEEPLY ALL OVER.

I WAS DRAGGED AGAINST ROCKS, AGAINST THE WALLS...

I'LL BE WITH YOU... SOON...

JUST WAIT, GAVNER...

GAZU
(GRSSH)

WE'LL GO INTO THAT DARK NIGHT ...

...TO-GETH-ER.

GO
(ZWOMM)

I WANT TO HELP YOU FIGHT THE VAMPANEZE, GAVNER!!

LET'S FIGHT TO- GETHER !!!

WHY ARE YOU WITH THE VAM- PANEZE?

KURDA? NO!

GACHI
(SHIVER)

GACHI

THANK GOODNESS...

GOSO
(RUSTLE)

GOSO

DEBBIE...

KATA

KATA
(SHIVER)

...OR I'LL FREEZE TO DEATH INSIDE THEM.

GU...
(GRRT)

BURU
(BRR)

BURU

GET RID OF THE WET CLOTHES QUICKLY...

MR. CREPSLEY TOLD ME WHAT TO DO IF THIS HAPPENED...

BIRI

BIRIRI
(RRIIP)

THEY'RE STILL THERE...

...THE BURN SCARS...

GUGU
CHRGH

RRGH
...

GU
...

ALL MY FRIENDS ...

MR. CREPS-LEY, HARKAT ...

JIWA
(DRIP)

IT LOOKS MILES AWAY.

THERE'S THE MOUN-TAIN.

IN THIS TERRIBLE STATE...

ZUZU (SLIDE)

WHY AM I EVEN WALKING...?

...AND BACK TO VAMPIRE MOUNTAIN, NO LESS...

DOSHA (THWOMP)

THERE'S NO SENSATION IN MY NERVES...

ZUKU ZUKUN (DRAG)

I CAN'T FEEL PAIN ANY-MORE... JUST THE COLD.

I'M JUST TOO TIRED... I CAN'T GO ON.

AM I DONE NOW, GAVNER? CAN I GIVE UP FOR GOOD?

YOU'VE GOT A MORE IMPORTANT ROLE THAN FIGHTING NOW, DARREN.

AWOO!!

AWOO!!

AWOO!!

I'M AT...MY... LIMIT...

EATEN ALIVE...

COULD THERE BE A MORE AWFUL WAY TO DIE?

A SQUIRREL COULD KNOCK ME OUT, IN MY CONDITION.

IS IT GOING... TO EAT ME?

HA HA

SOME-THING'S COMING.

ALL THAT'S LEFT...IS TO WAIT FOR THE MOMENT...

RED... NOSE...

THAT WHINE...

WHINE...

WHINE...

LICKING ITS PREY CLEAN BEFORE IT EATS?

WHAT'S IT DOING...?

PERO

PERO (LICK)

......?

GYU (HRRG)

NO WAY... IT CAN'T BE...

I NEVER THOUGHT I'D SEE YOU AGAIN...

R-RUDI? IS THAT YOU?

AWOOO!

BURU BURU (SHIVER)

BIG TROUBLE... I'VE BEEN THROUGH A LOT.

I'M IN BIG TROUBLE, RUDI.

PYON PYON (CHOP)

LOOK HOW YOU'VE GROWN...

GORO
(ROLL)

STREAK!

GASA
(RUSTLE)

ZA
(ZSHH)

MOZOZO
(NUZZLE)

I CAN FEEL
THE BLOOD
FLOWING
THROUGH MY
BODY AGAIN.

TOKUN

TOKUN
(THUMP)

THEY'RE
SO WARM
...

SIGH
...

I CAN'T GO ON, STREAK...

IT'S NO USE.

グ!! グ!!

GUGU (MMPH)

YEOW!!

GAPU (CHOMP)

ガブ

I'M STANDING...

STAY BACK, YOU NO-GOOD—

STOP IT!

THIS MUST BE STREAK'S FAMILY.

IT'S A PACK OF WOLVES.

GURURURU.
(GRRRR)

PIKU
(TWITCH)

RUDI?

TSUN TSUN (POKE)

YOU CAN'T MEAN —!!

HUH ?!

YOU WANT ME TO DRINK ?!

I CAN'T !!

KYAN (YIP)

YIP

GEEZ!

GUI (SHOVE)

CHAPTER 46:
THE TRAITOR'S PLOT

...AND THE COLD NO LONGER CUT ME TO THE BONE.

MY PAINS HAD FINALLY EASED...

IT HAD BEEN PERHAPS A WEEK SINCE I JOINED STREAK'S PACK.

I RECOVERED ENOUGH STRENGTH THAT I COULD GO HUNTING WITH THE PACK.

AS A HALF-VAMPIRE, I WAS FASTER THAN THE WOLVES, AND MY SERVICES WERE IN GREAT DEMAND.

IF IT WASN'T FOR THE WOLVES, I WOULDN'T BE ALIVE NOW.

MY VERY LIFE IS THANKS TO THEM.

STREAK HELPED FEED ME AS MY STRENGTH RETURNED...

...BRINGING ME MEAT AND BERRIES TO EAT.

DOSA (THUD)

THE FEW DAYS THAT I COULD BARELY MOVE AND HAD TO LAP AT THE MOTHER WOLF'S TEAT WERE LIKE A BAD DREAM BY THEN.

WE MOVED AROUND A LOT, AS WAS THE WOLVES' WAY.

THEY SHARE MANY SIMILARITIES WITH VAMPIRES.

HII ZA

HII ZA (ZSH)

THEIR GESTURES BEGAN TO MAKE SENSE TO ME.

I GRADUALLY LEARNED TO UNDERSTAND THE WOLVES' ACTIONS.

THE WOLVES SEEMED ABLE TO UNDERSTAND EVERYTHING I SAID.

HA-HA, YOU'VE GOT SNOW ON YOUR SNOUT.

AT TIMES, WHEN I CAUGHT A GLIMPSE OF VAMPIRE MOUNTAIN...

YOU DON'T WANT ME TO GO?

WHAT'S THAT, RUDI?

UUUU (GRRRR)

...MY LEGS WOULD SHIVER UNCONTROLLABLY.

KATA

KATA (SHIVER)

YOU MUST BE WORRIED.

KUUN (WHINE)

IT'S ALL RIGHT, RUDI. I'M NOT GOING BACK YET. IN FACT, I CAN'T GO BACK.

I MUST RETURN TO THE MOUNTAIN AT SOME POINT... BUT...

...BUT THE SENTENCE FOR BREAKING THE RULES OF THE VAMPIRES IS DEATH.

I CAN'T JUST IGNORE THE ISSUE OF KURDA AND THE VAMPANEZE...

...ONLY TO FIND THAT KURDA HAD ALLIED THE PRINCES AGAINST ME.

I MIGHT TELL THEM ABOUT THE VAMPANEZE...

I MADE EXCUSES TO MYSELF NOT TO LEAVE.

ONCE I'VE RECOVERED A LITTLE BIT MORE STRENGTH...

A LITTLE BIT LONGER...

WHY DID HE HAVE TO DIE...?

GUSHI (SQUISH)

HE WAS BRAVE AND LOYAL...

...WARM-HEARTED, AND A FRIEND TO ALL VAMPIRES.

WHY DID YOU KILL HIM, KURDA?

KUUN (WHINE)

GYUUU (SQUEEZE)

THANKS, RUDI...

PERO (CLICK)

PERO

...STREAK TOOK ME OUT FOR A HUNT, JUST THE TWO OF US.

ONE NIGHT, PERHAPS BECAUSE HE SENSED I WAS FEELING DOWN...

ZUSHA
(ZSHH)

THIS WASN'T LIKE THE USUAL HUNTS— WE WERE IN SEARCH OF SPORT, NOT PREY.

UNLIKE THE GROUP HUNTS, WE WERE FREE TO LOLLOP ABOUT AS WE PLEASED!

クン
KUN

クン KUN
(SNIFF)

WHAT'S THE MATTER, STREAK?

GASA

GASA
(RUSTLE)

ガサ

ガサ

クン
KUN

クン
KUN

ARE THOSE... PEOPLE OVER THERE...?

......!

?

AND ARRA?!

MR. CREPSLEY!!

SFX: GURURU (GRRR)

THEY COULD BE LOOKING FOR ME!

KURDA
!!!!

HAA
HAA
CHUFF?

ドクン
DOKUN
(THUMP?)

DOKUN

DOKUN

...BUT WHAT ARE THEY SAYING?

I CAN HEAR VOICES ON THE WIND...

I WISH TO LOCATE HIS BODY AND CREMATE HIM FITTINGLY.

...BUT I WOULD LIKE TO KEEP SEARCHING.

PROB-ABLY NOT...

DO YOU THINK WE'LL FIND HIM, LARTEN?

ズ...
ZUMU
(ZHUNF?)

YOU HAVE A POINT, BUT STILL...

EVEN THE TOUGHEST VAMPIRE HAS HIS LIMITS.

THE BOY IS TOUGH.

OF COURSE, HE MIGHT STILL BE ALIVE.

WE KNOW HE FELL INTO THE STREAM AND DID NOT EMERGE.

WE TRACED HIS PATH THROUGH THE TUNNELS.

...OR DARREN FELL IN TRYING TO SAVE HIM.

EITHER HE FELL INTO THE STREAM TRYING TO SAVE DARREN...

...BUT GAVNER HAS DISAPPEARED TOO.

I'D LOVE TO KNOW WHAT HAPPENED IN THOSE TUNNELS. IF DARREN HAD FALLEN IN BY HIMSELF, I COULD UNDERSTAND IT...

KACHA (KCHK)

AND WITHOUT ANY TRACE OF HIM IN THE STONE OF BLOOD, THERE CAN BE NO HOPE...

THE ABSENCE OF HIS MENTAL SIGNAL MEANS HE BREATHES NO LONGER.

AT LEAST WE KNOW THAT GAVNER IS DEAD.

I SEE...THE SITUATION IS STARTING TO MAKE SENSE.

KURDA, WORRIED THAT I MIGHT HAVE SURVIVED, OFFERED TO ASSIST.

MR. CREPSLEY IS LOOKING FOR SIGNS OF ME, AND ARRA IS TAGGING ALONG.

THEY'RE HEAVILY ARMED, LIKE KURDA.

HE MUST HAVE BROUGHT THE OTHER TWO.

HE MUST HAVE TALKED THEM INTO HIS WAY OF THINKING BEFORE THEY LEARNED THE WAYS OF THE CLAN.

GOKU (GULP)

THOSE VAMPIRES ARE YOUNG. KURDA LIKELY RECRUITED THEM HIMSELF.

KURDA HAS PUT TOGETHER HIS OWN ARMY, LOYAL ONLY TO HIM...

MATURE VAMPIRES VALUE HONOUR AND LOYALTY— THEY'D NEVER DREAM OF BEING IN CAHOOTS WITH A TRAITOR!!

DAR-REN'S AURA, ON THE OTHER HAND ...

THAT WAY HIS BETRAYAL WILL REMAIN A SECRET FOR GOOD ...

...HE AND HIS MEN WILL KILL ME, ARRA, AND MR. CREPSLEY.

IF I'M SPOTTED ALIVE...

...IS BEYOND MY GRASP, AND WE CANNOT LOOK FOR HIM WITH THE STONE OF BLOOD YET.

THE ODDS ARE STACKED AGAINST HIS BEING ALIVE, BUT UNTIL WE HAVE PROOF THAT HE IS DEAD, I SHALL NOT BE ABLE TO ACCEPT IT.

IT'S ODDLY COMFORTING...

...BUT HE'S STILL GOT HIS ELABORATE WAY OF TALKING.

IT FEELS LIKE YEARS SINCE I'VE HEARD THAT VOICE...

THERE IS KURDA'S INVESTITURE TO PREPARE FOR, COMING JUST THE NIGHT AFTER NEXT.

NO. IF WE DO NOT LOCATE HIS BODY TONIGHT, WE MUST ABANDON THE SEARCH.

IF HE CAN BE FOUND, WE'LL FIND HIM!

WE'LL GO ON SEARCHING.

34

YOUR PEOPLE EXPECT YOU TO SPEND TOMORROW FASTING AND PREPARING FOR THE INVESTITURE.

BUT DARREN—

...

NO. YOUR INVESTITURE AS A PRINCE TAKES PRECEDENCE ABOVE ALL ELSE.

SO KURDA'S GOING TO BE A VAMPIRE PRINCE...

INVESTI- TURE?

YOU ARE A TRUE FRIEND. THANK YOU.

I WON'T REST UNTIL WE KNOW FOR SURE IF DARREN IS ALIVE OR DEAD!

BUT THIS ISN'T THE END OF IT.

ZA
-(ZSHH)

ZA

I-GASASA

I OUGHT TO JUMP OUT AND STAB YOU DEAD WITH GAVNER'S KNIFE, RIGHT HERE AND NOW!!

PRE- TENDING TO BE UPSET!

THE HYPO- CRITE!

GASA
(RUSTLE)

......

GASA (KSSSH)

GASA

IT IS NOTHING, CYRUS.

IS SOMETHING WRONG?

LET'S GO.

I'D THOUGHT THEY JUST MEANT TO KILL AS MANY VAMPIRES AS THEY COULD AND TAKE OVER THE MOUNTAIN...

I HAD NEVER BEEN ABLE TO GRASP THE REASON FOR THE VAMPANEZE TO INVADE.

TOKUN (BA-BUMP)

TOKUN

KURDA'S GOING TO BE A PRINCE.

SORRY ABOUT THAT, STREAK...

HA HA...

SFX: UUUU (RRRRH...)

SIGH...

36

THEY COULD TRACK HIM WITH THE STONE OF BLOOD.

OF COURSE...

EVEN THE STONE... ...CANNOT FIND DARREN.

NO, THEIR GOAL MUST BE SOMETHING ELSE.

WHY GO TO ALL THAT RISK OVER A BUNCH OF CAVES?

...BUT THERE ARE MANY VAMPIRES WHO DIDN'T ATTEND THE COUNCIL.

THEY WOULD HAVE COME HERE AND SOUGHT REVENGE.

THE STONE OF BLOOD !!!

AND ONLY A VAMPIRE PRINCE CAN OPEN THE DOORS TO THE HALL.

BUT THE STONE IS MAGICALLY PROTECTED IN THE HALL OF PRINCES.

NOT ONLY THAT, THE STONE CAN SUPPOSEDLY BE USED TO SAVE THE VAMPIRES FROM THE DREADED LORD OF THE VAMPANEZE.

IF THAT'S TRUE, IT'S THE ONE THING THAT STANDS BETWEEN THE VAMPANEZE AND TOTAL VICTORY!!

ONLY A VAMPIRE PRINCE!

WITH IT, THE VAMPANEZE COULD DESTROY THE VAMPIRES AT WILL!

IT COULD BE USED TO LOCATE ALMOST ANY VAMPIRE ON THE PLANET.

HA (GASP)

THE CEREMONY FOR HIS INVESTITURE TOMORROW IS THE FINAL TIME LIMIT TO SAVE THE VAMPIRE RACE!

KURDA CAN'T BE ALLOWED TO GET HIS HANDS ON THE STONE OF BLOOD.

CHAPTER 47:
MAGDA THE GUIDE

THANK YOU FOR LETTING ME BE A MEMBER OF THE PACK.

I MADE UP MY MIND TO LEAVE THE WOLF PACK AND RETURN TO VAMPIRE MOUNTAIN.

...I'VE GOT TO GO.

WELL...

SFX: HA (PANT) HA

LET GO, RUDI. THAT HURTS.

I'VE BEEN TOO COWARDLY TO SAY GOOD-BYE UNTIL NOW.

IT'S TIME FOR ME TO MOVE ON.

UUUUU (GRRRR)

YOU NEED TO GROW UP BIG AND STRONG, JUST LIKE STREAK.

KUUN... (WHINE)

I DOUBT WE'LL EVER MEET AGAIN, RUDI...

...YOU WANT ME TO FOLLOW?

WHAT'S THAT...?

UOU (WOOF)

ZUMU...
(GISSH)

FUI
(CHMPH!)

KYUUUN

UOU

IT'S THE OLD SHE-WOLF WHO LIVES AT THE EDGES OF THE PACK...

IT MAKES NO SENSE...

UN-LESS—!!

OON (CAWOOO)

IS HE ASKING HER THE WAY TO THE MOUNTAIN?

WHAT IS STREAK ASKING OF THIS CRUSTY OLD SHE-WOLF?

GORO (ROLL)

GORO

UUUU (GRRR) UOU (WOOF)

YOU KNOW HOW TO GET INSIDE!!

BUT I CAN'T GET INSIDE THE FRONT GATE WITHOUT BEING SPOTTED BY THE OTHER VAMPIRES!!

THAT MUST BE IT! I KNOW HOW TO GET THERE.

...I MIGHT BE ABLE TO SNEAK IN!!

HOWEVER, IF THIS OLD WOLF KNOWS OF OLDER, LESS-USED PASSAGES...

STREAK!!

KYAN (GYAP)

KO (WHAK)

PLEASE, I NEED YOUR HELP!

CAN YOU TAKE ME THERE?

...BUT I'VE SIMPLY GOT TO MEET WITH THE PRINCES. IT'S TOO IMPORTANT.

SORRY TO PUSH YOU LIKE THIS...

ヨロ
(TREMBLE)

クゥン
(WHINE)

THANK YOU FOR EVERYTHING!!!

BYE, RUDI! BYE, EVERYONE!!

オオオン
(AWOOOO)

WE SURGED THROUGH THE FOREST, ACROSS SNOW AND ROCKS...

...MAKING GREAT TIME.

ビョォォォォォ
—BYOOO
(WHOOOSH)

STREAK AND TWO YOUNG MALE WOLVES JOINED THE OLD SHE-WOLF AND I ON OUR JOURNEY TO VAMPIRE MOUNTAIN.

ZEH (CHUFF?)

SAY, CAN I CALL YOU "MAGDA"?

IT'S MY GRAND-MOTHER'S NAME.

ZAZA (STOMP)

AH!

GA (SNAP)

I COULD CARRY YOU TO THE—

IS IT HARD?

FURA (SLUMP)

HA HA...

OKAY...I GUESS YOU'RE STRONG ENOUGH TO CON-TINUE.

WE TOOK SHELTER IN A SMALL TUNNEL AND WAITED FOR DAWN.

SOME-HOW, WE MANAGED TO REACH THE FOOT OF THE MOUNTAIN BY DUSK.

POOR MAGDA'S STUBBORN, BUT IN BAD SHAPE.

I FEEL GUILTY FOR DRAGGING HER ALONG ...

WE STAYED PUT AT NIGHT, AS THE VAMPIRES AND VAMPANEZE WOULD BE MOST ACTIVE THEN.

LET'S GET MOVING!!

KURDA'S INVESTITURE IS TONIGHT!!

ZASHI (ZSSH)

YORO (PLOD)

WE CAN FIND IT ON OUR OWN...

YOU DON'T HAVE TO KEEP GOING, MAGDA.

PYON (HOP)

PYON

YOTA (PLOD)

YOTA

...A NATURAL TUNNEL, NARROW AND UNUSED BY ANY VAMPIRE.

AS I SUSPECTED, MAGDA HAD GUIDED US TO A HIDDEN OPENING...

7

WE'RE IN A LARGER CHAMBER NOW...

...BUT SHE NEVER STOPPED HER PLODDING GAIT.

MAGDA LOOKED READY TO TOPPLE OVER AND DIE...

DID SHE ONCE WANDER INSIDE THEM, DRAWN BY THE SCENT OF FOOD?

WHEN DID MAGDA FIND OUT ABOUT THESE TUNNELS?

GASHA (KSHK)

GURURURU (GRRRR...)

PIKU (TWITCH)

ZEH (WHEEZE)

ZEH

KARAN (CLUNK)

OU (WOOF)

IS THERE SOME-THING... BACK THERE?

GU (HRG)

WHAT IS IT, STREAK?

UOU (WOOF)

!!!

BA!!
(LEAP)

WHO IS IT? A VAM-PANEZE?! NO...

SFX: GONYO (MUTTER) GONYO

ZUSHA
(THWAM)

GET OFF!!!!

GULP!!

GA
(WHOOSH)

9

A GUARDIAN OF THE BLOOD !!!

SFX: WOU (WOOF)

SFX: WON

WHAT DO YOU THINK YOU'RE DOING?!

SHH!

SHH!

WHAT'S THE BIG IDEA? WHAT DO YOU WANT ME TO...

GU (CHMPH)

HEY!

GU! (TUG)

SFX: GARURU UO (GRRRL RUFF)

OU
(WOOF)

GAUOU
(GROWR ROWR)

SO STREAK ISN'T GROWLING AT HIM?

IN THAT CASE, WHO OR WHAT IS OUT THERE?

GATA
(SHIVER)

GATA

GARURURU
(GRRRRR)

GURURURU...

ZA
(STOMP)

QUIET!! SHUT UP, YOU MONGRELS !!!

DOKI
(THUMP)

VAMPANEZE! AND THE ONE IN THE BACK WAS WITH KURDA...

I THINK HIS NAME WAS... GLALDA?

I OUGHT TO CUT THEM TO PIECES BEFORE THEY BRING THE VAMPIRES DOWN ON US!!

WE KEEP THINGS QUIET UNTIL THEN.

THE CEREMONY WILL BE STARTING SHORTLY.

NO, THEY'RE ONLY BARKING BECAUSE OF US. THEY'LL STOP ONCE WE LEAVE.

PE (PTUI)

I'VE BEEN ON EDGE TOO MUCH THESE DAYS.

OR MAYBE THAT'S JUST MY IMAGINA-TION.

GARURURU (GRRR)

BAKI (CRIK)

BOKI (CRAKK)

...IT HAS THE STINK OF VAM-PIRES ON IT.

BUT THIS ONE...

SFX: FU (HEH...)

50

HE'S GONE.

......

THEY ABANDONED ME TO MY DEATH IN THE HALL OF FINAL VOYAGE, SO WHY HELP ME NOW?

IT'S SO STRANGE...

I THOUGHT THE GUARDIANS OF THE BLOOD WERE...

YOU REALLY SAVED MY NECK THERE.

SIGH... THANKS.

I'VE GOT TO HURRY, OR KURDA'S INVESTITURE WILL START!

BUT NOW'S NOT THE TIME FOR THAT!

WOW...

I THINK WE'VE COME REALLY DEEP INTO THE MOUNTAIN!

THIS IS GREAT, MAGDA!

?F IE (WHEEZE)

ON AND ON, THE NARROW TUNNELS RAN.

WITH TIME, I COULD SENSE THE PRESENCE OF VAMPIRES, WORKING IN PREPARATION FOR THE FEAST AFTER THE CEREMONY.

C'MON, GUYS. WE'RE ALMOST THERE!

WHERE ARE YOU GOING, MAGDA?

MAG...

GOHHHHHH (WHOOOOSH)

THE SHAFT RISES SHARPLY FROM HERE.

52

I ONLY JUST NOTICED—NO, MAYBE I'VE BEEN PRETENDING NOT TO NOTICE THIS WHOLE TIME...

MAG... DA...

SHE DIDN'T WANT TO STRUGGLE ALONG WITH THE PACK UNTIL DEATH CLAIMED HER.

SHE CHOSE TO DIE BEING USEFUL TO SOMEONE.

MAGDA HAD KNOWN WHEN SHE STARTED THAT THE JOURNEY WOULD PROVE TOO MUCH FOR HER.

SHE CHOSE TO MAKE IT ALL THE SAME.

WAIT HERE AND WE'LL COLLECT YOU LATER.

IF YOU JUST LIE DOWN AND REST, I'M SURE YOU'LL...

YOU WERE PREPARED FOR THIS TO HAPPEN...

THANK YOU.

I, ON THE OTHER HAND...

MAGDA ACCEPTED DEATH CALMLY.

...RAN WHEN IT CAME TIME TO FACE MY END.

GA (CHRRG)

...SEARCHING FOR A SPOT TO QUIETLY LEAVE THIS WORLD BEHIND.

AND SHE HOBBLED AWAY INTO DARK-NESS...

54

THIS IS BRILLIANT, MAGDA...

YOU GUIDED ME TO THE VERY PLACE I NEEDED TO BE...

WHAT DOES IT MEAN TO DIE?

GARAN (CLUNK)

...THE HALL OF PRINCES.

GII (CREAK)

COME IN, THOMAS...

KON KON (TAP)

WE DO NOT HAVE TIME FOR...

THE INVESTITURE IS A MERE TWO HOURS AWAY.

I TOLD YOU NOT TO BOTHER KNOCKING.

GASHAA (KLAANG)

IS THAT... D-DARREN...?

THIS IS SUCH A JOY...

DARREN. OH, DARREN, MY BOY. YOU ARE ALIVE!

CHAPTER 48: INVESTITURE

ALAS, THE PRINCES HAVE SENTENCED YOU...

...TO DEATH.

NOT A VISION.

I CAN FEEL YOU. YOU ARE REAL!

YES...

YOUR TRAIL LED TO THE STREAM AND ENDED ABRUPTLY.

HOW DID YOU GET OUT?

YOU FLED.

I FIGURED AS MUCH.

I'M SORRY...

IT WAS A TERRIBLE MISTAKE.

BUT THAT'S GAVNER'S... WHY?

SU... (SHH)

AND I FENDED FOR MY LIFE WITH THIS.

I SWAM DOWN THE STREAM, OUT OF THE MOUN- TAIN.

HE WAS MURDERED ...

GAVNER'S DEAD.

YOU'D BETTER STAY SITTING, SEBA.

MUR... DER...?

PLEASE! YOU MUST BELIEVE ME!

YOU'RE THE ONLY ONE I CAN TURN TO NOW!

KURDA? TRULY?

HRGH...

BUT THIS... THIS IS IMPOSSIBLE...

SEBA!

FURA SWOOND

...EVEN THOUGH, IT SEEMS, I COULD NOT SEE THROUGH KURDA'S SCHEME.

I HAVE LIVED A VERY LONG LIFE. I CAN RECOGNIZE THE TRUTH WHEN IT IS REVEALED...

IF YOU KILL HIM, WE WON'T KNOW WHO ELSE HE'S WORKING WITH, OR WHY HE DID IT.

BE-SIDES...

NO, SEBA!!

I SHOULD SLIT THAT VILLAIN'S THROAT MYSELF!

GACHA CKCHAK

WHAT A WRETCHED WAY FOR GAVNER PURL TO MEET HIS END.

MURDERED BY THE MAN HE CONSIDERED A FRIEND...

GO (SHH)

...I WANT TO BLOW THE WHISTLE ON KURDA MYSELF.

...JUST HOW MUCH PAIN HE'S CAUSED.

I WANT TO MAKE SURE KURDA UNDER-STANDS...

YES, AND BECAUSE I MADE A PROMISE TO GAVNER.

BUT THAT'S NOT ALL.

TO PUNISH HIM FOR WHAT HE HAS DONE?

I WANT HIM TO KNOW HOW MUCH HE'S HURT ME...

HE SAVED MY LIFE.

I HATE HIM, SEBA, BUT I STILL THINK OF HIM AS A FRIEND.

YOU ARE A TRUE, COURA-GEOUS VAMP-IRE.

YOU HAVE OVERCOME GREAT ODDS TO BE HERE.

SFX: PON (PAT)

...BUT I WANT HIM TO SEE THAT I DON'T GET ANY PLEASURE OUT OF EXPOSING HIM AS A TRAITOR.

MAYBE IT DOESN'T REALLY MAKE SENSE...

...DARREN SHAN.

LARTEN WILL BE PROUD OF YOU...

THE PRINCES WILL SEE NO ONE UNTIL THE CEREMONY. THEY WILL STAY SEALED IN THE HALL OF PRINCES.

LISTEN CLOSELY, DARREN. THE ONLY OPPORTUNITY TO REVEAL KURDA'S TREACHERY IS IN THE MIDDLE OF HIS INVESTITURE!

ZAWA

ZAWA (MURMUR)

THIS CEREMONY IS THE ONE TIME IT IS ALLOWED TO BRING WEAPONS INTO THE CHAMBER.

THE PROBLEM WILL BE THAT EVERYONE SHALL BE ARMED.

STUBBORN WOLF.

I THOUGHT I TOLD YOU NOT TO FOLLOW ...

ANY ONE OF THE CROWD COULD BE A TRAITOR ...

I WILL POSITION SOME OF MY STAFF NEARBY.

WE WILL GUARD YOUR LIFE!

...WITH ORDERS TO KILL YOU ON SIGHT. MEASURES MUST BE TAKEN.

SFX: KOKU (NOD)

THEN, I SURVIVED THE FEROCIOUS STREAM...

IF I HADN'T FAILED THE TRIALS, I NEVER WOULD HAVE LEARNED OF THE VAMPANEZE PLOT.

IS THIS THE LUCK OF THE VAMPIRES... OR DESTINY?

FINALLY, MAGDA KNEW JUST WHERE TO LEAD ME...

...AND WAS RESCUED IN THE NICK OF TIME BY RUDI AND STREAK.

...CONSPIRING TO MAKE IT HAPPEN THIS WAY...

I'M NOT ONE TO BELIEVE IN FATE, BUT IT'S ALMOST AS IF SOME GREAT UNSEEN POWER IS BRINGING THIS ABOUT...

AND NOW IT BEGINS!!

GUKU
(GRRK)

SUUU
(SHHH)

...OF TRUTH!!!

THE MOMENT...

ONE OF THEM GOT LOOSE!

CALM YOUR-SELVES!!

AA AH H!!

ドゥ
DOYO

ドゥ…
DOYO (MURMUR)

シ!!
KA (TAK)

NOT NOW !!

HOW DID...

DARREN? WHAT IS GOING ON?

GOTO (TUNK)

PLEASE SET ME DOWN.

I'LL TELL YOU ABOUT IT LATER.

I'M SORRY...

......

SU... (SHH)

TA

TA (TEK)

SIRE!!

WHAT'S GOING ON HERE?!

YOU'RE PART OF THIS CHAOS, SEBA?

GIRI GGRRD

I WOULD STRONGLY ADVISE THAT YOU LET DARREN SPEAK!!

THOSE WHO RAISED WEAPONS AGAINST DARREN ARE NOT OUR ALLIES!!

SIRE, YOU WILL UNDERSTAND ONCE YOU HAVE HEARD WHY DARREN HAS RETURNED TO OUR MIDST!!

NEVER BEFORE HAS ANYONE INTERRUPTED THE INVESTITURE OF A PRINCE!!

REMOVE THEM BOTH FROM THE HALL!!

ENOUGH, SEBA! WHY DO YOU INSIST ON TAKING THE SIDE OF THIS COWARD?!

SUCH SLANDER!!

HOW DARE YOU!!

...NO ONE HAS EVER SOUGHT TO INVEST A TRAITOR BEFORE, EITHER!!

DOYO (MURMUR)

NO, WAIT!

IT MAY BE TRUE THAT NO ONE HAS INTERRUPTED AN INVESTITURE BEFORE.

BUT I SAY...

IT'S BAD ENOUGH THAT A BOY VIOLATES OUR LAWS AND CUSTOMS ...

THIS IS A GRIM NIGHT.

BIRI

BIRI (WINCE)

STOP THIS !!!!

ENOUGH !!!

BUT HE CALLED KURDA A TRAITOR!

...BEHAVE LIKE A PACK OF BARBARIANS ...

...BUT WHEN FULLY BLOODED VAMPIRES WHO SHOULD KNOW BETTER ...

...TO SUFFER THE FATE HE DESERVES!!

WERE IT UP TO ME, ARROW, I'D HAVE THIS BOY BOUND AND GAGGED AND TAKEN TO THE HALL OF DEATH...

...THEN I, FOR ONE, AM LOATH TO DISREGARD HIM.

IF SEBA NILE SAYS WE SHOULD LISTEN TO WHAT HE HAS TO SAY...

THANK YOU, SIRE ...

...HAS SPOKEN UP ON THE BOY'S BEHALF.

BUT ONE WE ALL KNOW, TRUST, AND ADMIRE...

THAT'S RIGHT!

KILL HIM!

IN-DEED !!

...BUT MAKE IT QUICK.

SAY YOUR PIECE, DARREN...

LET'S SEE IF THIS IS QUICK ENOUGH!

OKAY!

AT THIS VERY MOMENT, DOZENS OF VAMPANEZE LURK IN THE TUNNELS BENEATH US...

...WAITING FOR JUST THE RIGHT MOMENT TO ATTACK!!!

GAVNER PURL, THE VAMPIRE GENERAL GONE MISSING, WAS MURDERED.

...AS WELL AS THE MURDER OF GAVNER...

AND THE VAMPANEZE INFILTRA- TION...

...WERE THE ACTS OF ONE SINGLE VAMPIRE...

KURDA
SMAHLT
...

...THE
TRAITOR.

KURDA HAS BETRAYED ...

CHAPTER 49: ACCUSATION

...THE ENTIRE VAMPIRE CLAN!!!

1

AND YOU ARE CERTAIN WE WILL TRUST YOUR WORD?

THESE ARE GRAVE CHARGES TO BRING.

DO YOU THINK I'D DO THAT FOR NO GOOD REASON?

BY RETURNING AFTER FAILING THE TRIALS, I'VE CONDEMNED MYSELF TO EXECUTION.

NOT TO MENTION THOSE WHO ATTACKED HIM ON SIGHT...

I AGREE, BUT IF HE WISHED TO FOOL US, HE WOULD HAVE CHOSEN A LESS FANTASTIC STORY.

THIS MAKES NO SENSE...

NO, I THINK KURDA PLANS TO WAIT UNTIL HE IS INVESTED...

AND THEIR AIMS? WILL THEY ATTACK US?

AT LEAST THIRTY— POSSIBLY MORE.

HOW MANY VAMPANEZE ARE DOWN THERE?

...TO LET THEM INTO THE HALL OF PRINCES AND SEIZE CONTROL OF THE STONE OF BLOOD!!

YOU DON'T DENY THE CHARGE?!

AT THIS MOMENT— NOTHING.

......

BUT I CANNOT BELIEVE KURDA WOULD BETRY US.

GU CHRRG!

ONLY A PRINCE WOULD BE CAPABLE OF OPENING THE HALL OF PRINCES TO ANOTHER...

WHAT DO YOU HAVE TO SAY IN REBUTTAL OF DARREN'S CLAIMS?

I DO NOT.

SHA
(SHK)

NO!
STOP
HIM!

DOSA
(THUD)

GUI
(SHOVE)

AND
DO NOT
LET HIM
TAKE
HIS
OWN
LIFE.

KEEP
HIM
ALIVE
UNTIL
WE HAVE
TIME TO
INTER-
ROGATE
HIM!!

THERE
WILL BE
TIME
FOR
TRAI-
TORS
LATER!

SEBA IS
RIGHT. THE
VAMPANEZE
MUST BE
PUT TO THE
SWORD!

WITH RESPECT,
SIRES, WOULD IT
NOT MAKE MORE
SENSE TO FOCUS
ON THE VAMPANEZE
BEFORE WE
EXECUTE OUR
OWN?

WE WILL SEE THE PRESENT DANGER DEALT WITH!

WHEN WE HAVE DECIDED ON AN IMMEDIATE COURSE OF ACTION, WE SHALL INFORM YOU.

オギ!!
(CRAHH)

WE WILL RETIRE TO THE HALL OF PRINCES WITH DARREN!

RIGHT...

COME, DARREN.

KURDA'S TREACHERY, MY TRIP DOWN THE STREAM, MY RESCUE BY THE WOLVES...

I TOLD THE PRINCES EVERY DETAIL OF MY STORY.

AND THERE COULD VERY WELL BE MORE OF THEM...

YES, I DID.

DID YOU SPOT THOSE TWO TRAITORS IN THE CAVE?

...AND THEN MY SIGHTING OF KURDA WITH HIS FOLLOWERS.

I SUPPOSE THAT MEANS I HAVE TO STAY BEHIND AND GUARD THE HALL.

SO YOUNG AND BLOODTHIRSTY.

...UNTIL EVERY LAST ONE HAS BEEN DROPPED ON THE STAKES IN THE HALL OF DEATH.

BUT NOW, WE'VE GOT VAMPANEZE TO KILL. I WON'T REST...

SFX: GOKIKI (CRIKK)

...NOT SET IN MOTION A SERIES OF WITCH HUNTS.

BUT THIS IS THE TIME TO PULL TOGETHER AS ONE ...

IT'S A DEAL.

EASY, MY FRIEND. LEAVE ENOUGH FOR ME TO WHET MY BLADE ON!

YOU ARE TOO KIND.

HEH HEH HEH...

......

WE'LL LET YOU MOP UP THE STRAGGLERS.

ONE OF US WILL RELIEVE YOU BEFORE THE END.

GUGU (KRRRK)

ZAWA ZAWA (MURMUR)

DARREN WILL GO WITH THEM TO SHOW THEM THE INHABITED CAVES.

BUT THAT COMES LATER. FIRST, LET US SUMMON OUR BEST TRACKERS.

YES!

DA (DASH)

DARREN!!

WE WILL BE ARRANGING A SEARCH PARTY TO FIND THE VAMPANEZE!

HAR-KAT!

NOT EXACTLY. I GAVE MYSELF UP.

DID THEY... CATCH YOU?

WHAT ARE... YOU DOING... HERE?

HE WOULD NOT EVEN TELL ME THE TRUTH OF YOUR ESCAPE.

BUT WHY DID YOU BRING MADAM OCTA?

I WANTED TO...TAKE HER AND... ESCAPE WITH YOU... THIS TIME.

BUT... WHY?

DON'T ASK ME TO EXPLAIN IT NOW.

I'VE GOT TO GUIDE A SEARCH PARTY TO THE TUNNELS WHERE THE VAMPANEZE WERE.

I'M SORRY I RAN AWAY.

BUT DO NOT CHASTISE YOURSELF TOO MUCH.

SO YOU SHOULD BE. IT WAS NOT LIKE YOU, DARREN.

...WE WOULD NEVER HAVE BEEN ALERTED TO KURDA OR THE VAMPANEZE.

I SAY IT WAS FATE. HAD HE NOT FLED...

I AM MORE TO BLAME FOR LETTING THEM SUBJECT YOU TO THE TRIALS IN THE FIRST PLACE.

THANKS.

...KEEP TIME...ON A HEART-SHAPED... WATCH...

THE HANDS OF FATE...

NOW, LET'S GET YOU IN SOME REAL CLOTHES FOR THIS SEARCH.

I KNEW YOU WOULD NOT DESERT US, DARREN!

(GASH) (SQUEEZE)

OUCH!

IT WAS A POOR DECISION YOU WERE BOUND TO CORRECT!!

I WAS SURE YOU'D RETURN ONCE YOU HAD TIME TO THINK THINGS THROUGH!

GA HA HA!

NOW THAT YOU MENTION IT...NO, I DIDN'T!

I BET YOU DIDN'T BET ON ME RETURNING, THOUGH.

YES. I'M BORROWING GAVNER'S.

THAT KNIFE... IS IT...?

THANKS, ARRA... BUT I'VE ALREADY GOT ONE!

IF YOU HAVE TO USE IT, DON'T HESITATE.

TAKE THIS, DARREN.

WHEN I LED THE PARTY BACK TO THE ORIGINAL CAVE, IT WAS DESERTED.

UNTIL I CAN AVENGE HIM.

IT DIDN'T TAKE THEM LONG TO UNCOVER EVIDENCE OF VAMPANEZE, HOWEVER.

THEY SURE COVERED THEIR TRACKS.

YES, BUT IT WAS VAMPANEZE, ALL RIGHT.

...ALL RIGHT.

WE'LL BE BACK WHEN WE FIND THE VAMPANEZE.

WE BROUGHT YOU DOWN TO SHOW US THE CAVE.

YES, BUT I WANT TO COME WITH YOU.

CAN YOU FIND YOUR WAY BACK TO THE HALLS FROM HERE, DARREN?

HARKAT HAS BEEN TAKING GOOD CARE OF YOUR SPIDER.

MADAM OCTA LOOKS WELL!

DAR-REN, YOU'RE BACK!

SEBA, HAR-KAT.

SPEAKING WITH THE PRINCES.

ZAWA (MURMUR)

ZAWA

WHERE IS MR. CREPS-LEY?

...BUT THERE'S STILL MY FAILURE IN THE TRIALS TO DEAL WITH.

YOU MAY WIND UP WITH HER YET. I SEEM TO HAVE WON BACK MY HONOUR...

I HAD A FEEL-ING YOU MIGHT BE BACK.

HE OFFERED TO GIVE HER TO ME WHEN YOU DISAPPEARED, BUT I TOLD HIM TO HANG ON TO HER.

...THEY WON'T PUNISH... YOU FOR... THAT NOW?

SURE-LY...

THEY ARE IN A LONG, NARROW CAVE NEAR THE EXTERIOR!

WE'VE DISCOVERED THE LOCATION OF THE VAMPANEZE!

ROUGHLY FORTY IN NUMBER!

REPORTING!

ZAWA

VANEZ AND ARRA ARE BACK!

THE GROUND IS STEEP WHERE THE TUNNEL OPENS OUT...

...AND WE CONFIRMED SENTRIES AT THE MOUTH.

...SO THEY CAN FLIT AWAY AND ESCAPE IF THEY HAVE TO.

THE EXIT TUNNEL RUNS STRAIGHT TO THE OUTSIDE...

PIKU (TWITCH)

YOU THINK THEY MIGHT BEAT US IN A FAIR FIGHT?

... WOULD BE TO SPRING A TRAP.

I BELIEVE THAT OUR BEST OPTION TO CATCH AND WIPE OUT ALL THE VAMPANEZE...

I THINK SO, SIRE.

I SEE. SO IT WOULD BE DIFFICULT TO CORNER THEM.

IN- DEED.

BUT THEY'VE PICKED THEIR POSITION EXPERTLY. ARRA?

NO, SIRE.

OUR SUPERIOR NUMBERS WILL LEAD TO EVENTUAL VICTORY, BUT THEY HAVE NOTHING TO LOSE.

WE WOULD BE LOOKING AT MASSIVE CASUALTIES FOR A CERTAINTY.

THE TUNNEL IS NARROW, AND WE'LL ONLY BE ABLE TO FIGHT THEM ONE-ON-ONE.

BUT NEITHER CAN WE TRAP THEM IN!

WE CANNOT FIGHT THEM HEAD-ON, AS THEY WILL EITHER ESCAPE OR KILL TOO MANY!

THEN WHAT OPTION DO WE HAVE, VANEZ?

HOW ABOUT A DIVERSION? COULD WE FLOOD OR SMOKE THEM OUT?

I'VE THOUGHT OF THAT, BUT THE LAYOUT MAKES IT DIFFICULT.

DON'T BELLOW AT ME IN THAT TONE...

ZU (CHRRM)

WOULD YOU RATHER WE WENT DOWN WITH A WHITE FLAG AND DISCUSSED PEACE TERMS?

GOGO (RUMBLE)

ZAWA

ZAWA

ZAWA

REMEMBER, MY DISLIKE FOR THE VAMPANEZE IS NO LESS THAN YOURS, SIRE!!

COWARD!!

ZAWA

I'M ONLY SAYING IT WILL BE A PYRRHIC VICTORY IF WE FIGHT ONE-ON-ONE!

ZAWA (MUTTER)

IT IS THE FIRST RULE OF WARFARE.

NEVER WEAKEN YOURSELF IRREPARABLY WHILE DESTROYING YOUR ENEMIES.

IF WE DEFEAT THE VAMPANEZE, BUT LOSE MANY OF OUR OWN, IT WILL BE A WORTHLESS VICTORY.

PYRRHIC VICTORY?

IT IS WHEN THE PRICE OF WINNING IS TOO HIGH.

AFTER ALL THIS, I CAN'T GET REVENGE FOR GAVNER...

GU... (CHRG)

WE COULD NOT ALLOW OUR MEN TO PERISH IN NUMBER ALL FOR THE SAKE OF HONOUR.

BUT PRIDE MUST BE CHECKED AND REASON OBEYED.

ZAWA ZAWA (MURMUR)

NOR DO I.

THEY DON'T LIKE THIS.

GAYA GAYA (YAMMER)

HEY!

PISHUN (PSHOOT)

AWW, SHE... ATE IT ALL...

MUSHA (CHOMP)

MUSHA

NO, MADAM... LET GO ...

EXCUSE ME...

GAYA

KEEP QUIET, DARREN!

GAYA

ZAWA

GEKON (AHEM)

GOHON (ER-ERM)

KOHO (AHEM)

...BUT I THINK I KNOW HOW TO DISTRACT THE VAMPANEZE.

SPEAK TO THE CROWD.

AND AN IDEA IS WHAT WE NEED.

UM, IT'S JUST AN IDEA...

IS THIS TRUE, DAR-REN?

BA
(SPIN)

JI...
CHMMO

GOKU
(GULP)

I WOULD NOW LIKE TO OUTLINE...

...MY PLAN!!

EVEN PARIS WAS LAUGHING.

HE SAID THAT THERE WAS NO BETTER SCHEME TO WIPE OUT THE VAMPANEZE.

DARREN, THIS IS EASILY THE MOST CUNNING PLAN I HAVE HEARD IN AGES.

CHAPTER 50:
THE BATTLE BEGINS

LEAVE THE REST TO US.

JUST FOCUS ON YOUR PART OF THE PLAN, DARREN.

WOR-RIED? I'M MORE CON-CERNED FOR YOUR SAKE...

...LAR-TEN.

THE FRONT LINE?!

HMPH.

VANEZ AND I ENLISTED FOR ARROW'S FIRST SQUAD.

ARE YOU FIGHTING TOO, ARRA?

I'VE GOT IT.

THIS PLAN'S SUCCESS RESTS ON YOUR EFFORTS.

IT'S UP TO YOU, DARREN.

BE CAREFUL, DARREN.

YOU WILL START FROM THE OUTSIDE.

SEBA AND I SHALL WORK WITHIN THE TUNNEL.

YOU TOO, ARRA.

LUCK TO YOU.

BUT NOW THE SUN IS SHINING ON IT.

THAT'S THE MOUTH OF THE TUNNEL THE VAMPANEZE ARE IN.

SFX: DOKI (BA-BUMP) DOKI

AND I'M THE ONLY HALF-VAMPIRE, CAPABLE OF MOVING UNDER DAYLIGHT.

WE MUST ATTACK BY DAY TO PREVENT THEM FROM ESCAPING!

KOSO (SNEAK)

VEN-GEACE WILL BE YOURS, GAVNER!

OKAY... MADAM OCTA'S IN PLACE...

...COMMENCES NOW!!!!

OPERATION ARACHNID...

ALM OWN!

BAH...

NOT NOW! WHEN THE SIGNAL COMES.

WHEN ARE WE GONNA MOVE, GLALDA?!

I TOLD YOU NO! WAIT!

EVERYONE'S WORRIED! LET'S MOVE NOW!

IRA IRA (GRR)

IRA

CURSE YOU, KURDA... WHAT'S HAPPENING?

MOZO (RUSTLE)

MOZO

H-HEY... IS IT MY IMAGINATION, OR ARE THE WALLS... MOVING?

HUH?

WHAT'S WRONG?

AAAH!

SHOO! BEGONE!

OH... JUST A SPIDER.

KASA (SCUTTLE)

KASA

......

HOW LONG ARE WE GONNA BE STUCK IN...

WHAT'S HAPPEN-ING?!

AAAHH!!

AAAH!

EEEK!

WHAT ARE THEY ?!

THERE'RE MILLIONS OF THEM! WE'RE SUR-ROUNDED!

THEY'RE PUSHING IN FROM ALL SIDES!

CALM DOWN! ORDINARY MOUNTAIN SPIDERS CAN'T HURT YOU...

DON'T HIT OUR OWN KIND WITH YOUR WEAPONS!

TOO MANY...

THERE ARE TOO MANY OF THEM!

GABU (CHOMP)

BIKU (TWITCH)

BIKU

BITE! ATTACK!

WORKING TOGETHER TO CONTROL ALL THE SPIDERS IN THE MOUNTAIN, MR. CREPSLEY, SEBA, AND I SET THE CREATURES UPON THE VAMPANEZE!

THESE WERE SEBA'S BA'HALEN SPIDERS, NO ORDINARY CAVE ARACHNIDS.

ZUBA (FORTH)

EEE!

AAH!

THE VAMPANEZE, OVERWHELMED BY THE WAVE OF HUGE SPIDERS ...

...SOON MET THEIR NEXT TEST...

MADAM OCTA TOOK CHARGE OF THE OTHER SPIDERS.

SHE PATROLLED THE GROUP AND KEPT THEM IN LINE.

...THE VAMPIRE WAR PARTY, LED BY NONE OTHER THAN PRINCE ARROW!

ATTACK !!!

THE BATTLE IS ON...

OPERATION ARACHNID WAS A SUCCESS!

HE'S YOUNG FOR A VAMPANEZE.

HIS SKIN IS ONLY LIGHT PURPLE...

I NEVER EVEN CONSIDERED THE CONSEQUENCES OF THIS REVENGE!

KAHA CHACK

HE DESERVED TO DIE! HE'S EVIL!

BUT STILL, HE'S A MURDERER WHO DRINKS HUMAN BLOOD!

HOW DOES ONE SEPARATE THE RIGHT FROM WRONG WHERE KILLING IS CONCERNED? YOU CAN'T...

BUT EITHER WAY...I DON'T HAVE THE RIGHT TO DETERMINE THAT.

OOGYAAA (WAAAHH)

WAA (CRAAH)

FURA (FLUP)

IS IT BECAUSE I'M NOT A FULL VAMPIRE?

I CAN'T FATHOM WHAT'S GOING ON...

EVERYTHING LOOKS... WRONG.

THE VAMPIRES ARE SO GHOULISHLY SATISFIED BY THIS MASSACRE...

WHAT'S GOING ON?

I'VE KILLED ANOTHER MAN, WHO WAS SOMEONE ELSE'S FRIEND, SON, OR LOVER.

I'VE DONE THE SAME THING AS KURDA, WHOM I CURSED SO BITTERLY.

I CAN'T TELL WHAT'S RIGHT...FROM WHAT'S WRONG.

UWAAA (AAAH!)

FURA (FLUD)

GYAAA (AAAGH)

IT JUST DOESN'T MAKE SENSE ANYMORE, KURDA.

NICHA (SPLT)

!!

YOU SHOULDN'T BE HERE, DARREN! YOU OUGHT TO LEAVE!

HAA (CHUFF)

HAA

...OR SO I THOUGHT.

VANEZ?

THIS IS A GREAT SPORT TO US, DARREN. THE GREATEST...

GOSHI (RUB)

....

UNTIL NOW...

YOU WERE SMART ENOUGH TO SEE IT, AND DON'T FORGET THAT.

BUT YOU WERE ABLE TO SEE THE TRUTH, DARREN.

WE DON'T REALIZE WE'RE DESTROYING A PART OF OUR-SELVES.

THE VAMPANEZE WERE ONCE OUR BROTHERS.

...HE STARED RIGHT INTO MINE...

...WHEN MY EYES MET KURDA'S AS HE WAS TAKEN AWAY IN THE HALL...

YES, THE MO-MENT...

HE CARRIED ON A LONELY BATTLE, A SILENT WAR.

KURDA UNDER-STOOD THAT TOO, OF COURSE.

NOT UNTIL THE MOMENT I SAW IT.

AND I NEVER REALIZED KURDA'S PAIN.

106

GACHA (CLANK)

...AND AMID THE JEERS OF OUR BROTHERS...

...HE SIMPLY SMILED, SADLY AND APOLOGET- ICALLY...

YOU SHOULD LEAVE, DARREN. THIS IS WHERE THE TRULY DIRTY WORK BEGINS.

YOU'VE FUL- FILLED YOUR DUTY HERE.

WAOOO (RAHHH)

OH NO !!!

GASHA (GSHK)

ANOTHER PATH...BUT I THOUGHT THIS WAS A SINGLE TUNNEL...

HYUU (WHOOSH)

!!

A BREEZE?

HYOOO (WHOOSH)

FOR-
GIVE
ME...

I'VE GOT
THINGS TO
ACCOMPLISH
YET, WOMAN.

NO,
DAR-
REN...

STAY...
AWAY...

GO
GGRAHHD

I CAN STILL FEEL THAT SICKENING SENSATION IN MY HAND.

...WHAT SEPA-RATES RIGHT FROM WRONG.

I JUST DON'T KNOW ANYMORE...

I JUST CAN'T STAND BY...

BUT I CAN'T...

CHAPTER 51: LAST WILL

...AND LET ARRA BE KILLED BEFORE MY EYES!!!

CHAPTER 51:
LAST WILL

ZURU
(SLIP)

ONLY DIG-GING... YOUR OWN...

FOOLISH VAM-PIRES ...

HA... HA HA... HA HA HA...

... GRAVES ...

DOO
(WHAMM)

EVEN IN DEATH, MAY YOU BE TRIUMPHANT...

GAKU
(SLUMP)

ARRA
...!!

BURU
(SHIVER)

BURU

DAR—

HA (CHFF)

HA

...STUPID QUESTIONS.

TALK ABOUT ASKING...

DOES IT HURT, ARRA?

...FOR PUTTING MY FOOT IN MY MOUTH.

YOU ALWAYS SAID I HAD A TALENT...

DARREN...

THERE WILL BE PLENTY OF TIME FOR KISSING LATER...

...ANY SHAPE FOR IT...

I'D ASK YOU TO KISS ME, ONLY... I'M NOT IN...

MAYBE.

MAYBE...

HAH.

YOU PUT UP...A GOOD FIGHT. ALMOST GOT ME...

OF COURSE.

...DO YOU REMEMBER... WHEN I BEAT YOU...ON THE BARS?

...MY VENGEANCE...

THANK YOU FOR TAKING...

GAHA (GAAHK)

YOU HAVE GROWN... SO MUCH STRONGER... SINCE THE TRIALS...

HE'S A WORTHY VAMPIRE... HE'S EARNED... A REPRIEVE!!

DON'T LET THEM KILL HIM, LARTEN!!

THE REMAINING VAMPANEZE CALMLY, FIRMLY STOOD THEIR GROUND.

AS THE BATTLE DREW TO A CLOSE, THE INTENSITY ONLY GREW HIGHER.

...HOW TO WIN AND HOW TO DIE. THERE WAS NO IN-BETWEEN.

THEY ONLY KNEW TWO THINGS ...

BUT NOT A ONE OF THEM WOULD BOW AND SURRENDER.

THE OUTCOME WAS CLEAR TO ALL.

DOSHU COSHIKO

VANEZ

NOW IS THE TIME TO ACQUI-ESCE!!

YOU HAVE FOUGHT VALIANT-LY!!

MAY THE DEMONS TAKE YOU TO HELL!!!!!

I WOULD NEVER SURRENDER TO A VAMPIRE !!!

...AND THE BATTLE HAD BEEN WON BY THE VAMPIRES.

AND WITH THAT, THE LAST VAMPANEZE WAS KILLED...

THEY WEREN'T SO TOUGH!

HEY, I KILLED THIS FELLA!

GA-HA-HA! THIS IS BUT A SCRATCH!

BUT WAS IT REALLY FOR THE BEST, GAVNER?

YOU DID WELL, BOYS...

SEBA.

MIND IF I JOIN YOU?

BWA HA HA!

HA HA HA!

IT IS A GREAT SHAME ABOUT ARRA...

LARTEN IS DEVASTATED. HE STILL LOVED HER. IT WILL BE HARD FOR HIM TO BEAR.

MANY GAVE THEIR LIVES FOR THIS FIGHT.

YOU SHOULD NOT SAY THAT.

EVERYONE FIGHTING AND DYING OVER THIS ...

IT'S ALL SO STUPID ...

WE DIDN'T NEED TO COME DOWN HERE AND CUT THEM TO PIECES!

WE COULD HAVE DRIVEN THEM OFF!

THAT'S WHAT MAKES IT STUPID!

THIS BATTLE WAS HARSH, BUT UNAVOID- ABLE.

WE DID NOT WISH FOR IT TO HAPPEN. OUR HAND WAS FORCED.

EVEN I KILLED TWO OF THEM!

AND IT WAS MY PLAN THAT PAVED THE WAY FOR SO MUCH DEATH AND KILLING!

IT IS ALL RIGHT.

N-NO, I'M ONLY...

HEH. NOW YOU ARE SPEAKING LIKE KURDA.

BUT IF WE DON'T MAKE ANY ATTEMPTS AT BEFRIENDING THEM...

...WE'LL NEVER BE ABLE TO PREVENT THIS FROM HAPPENING AGAIN.

I KNOW...

...BUT IT IS POSSIBLE THAT THE NEXT GENERATION TO COME ALONG WILL.

I CAN NO LONGER CHANGE MY WAYS...

GA HA HA!

BWA HA HA HA!

PERHAPS YOU ARE RIGHT. I AM OLD AND STUCK IN THE PAST.

...OUT OF THE DARKNESS OF THE PAST AND INTO THE LIGHT.

SOMEONE MUST LEAD US NOW...

PACHI (WINK)

PERHAPS IT IS TIME FOR US TO CHANGE TOO.

I MUST ADMIT THAT THE WORLD HAS CHANGED.

KASASA
(SKITTER)

MOZO
(RUSTLE)

THIS IS ONE OF THE SURVIVORS, AND HE SHOWS NO SIGN OF LEAVING MADAM OCTA'S SIDE.

MANY OF THE SPIDERS WERE CRUSHED IN THE FIGHTING.

ONE OF BA'HALEN'S SPIDERS, WITH MADAM OCTA...

...I WAS ACTUALLY THINKING ALONG THE LINES OF FREEING HER. WHAT DO YOU SAY?

DARREN ...

MAYBE I SHOULD PUT HIM IN HER CAGE...

HUH?

PERHAPS HE IS SWEET ON HER. HO-HO!

126

YOU DO NOT WANT TO CHECK WITH LARTEN?

I THINK HE'S GOT BIGGER THINGS TO WORRY ABOUT.

OKAY. IT'S PROBABLY FOR THE BEST.

FREE...

LIVE LONG.

KOTO CTHULHO

GO.

YOU'RE FREE.

OUT OF YOUR CELL, KURDA SMAHLT.

PICHAN (SPLISH)

YOUR VAMPANEZE ALLIES HAVE ALL BEEN PUT TO THE SWORD.

GARARARA (CLANK CLANK)

THE BATTLE HAS ENDED WITH A VAMPIRE VICTORY.

YOUR SENTENCING IS NIGH.

CHAPTER 52:
KURDA'S CONFESSION

PASA
(FLAP)

KA

KA
(TAK)

DAR-
REN
...

MR...
CREPS-
LEY...

I'M HAVING TROUBLE.

COULD YOU NOT SLEEP?

ARRA'S...

ARRA IS...

I THOUGHT SHE WAS GOING TO MAKE IT. I KNEW THE WOUND WAS FATAL...

...BUT SHE LASTED SUCH A LONG TIME, DEFYING THE ODDS, I BEGAN TO BELIEVE SHE WOULD LIVE.

SORRY...

YOU HEARD THE NEWS?

YEAH.

EVEN AFTER SHE DIED, SHE LAY THERE FOR MINUTES, SERENE IN MY EMBRACE, SMILING BLANKLY AT ME.

SHE CLUNG TO LIFE AS LONG AS SHE COULD.

SHE DID NOT SAY MUCH ONCE SHE LEFT THE CAVE...

JIWA (DRIP)

HOW CAN I SLEEP?

HAVE YOU HAD ANY SLEEP?

I COULD NOT HEAR... HER LAST WORDS...

SHE SPOKE... TOO SOFTLY...

THERE ARE THE INQUISITIONS TO PREPARE FOR. I WILL NOT MISS KURDA'S SENTENCING...

...NOT IF I HAVE TO FORSAKE SLEEP FOREVER!

YOU DID WELL IN THE CAVE, DARREN.

YOU FOUGHT BRAVELY.

I WAS PROUD OF YOU.

GUZU (KNIFE)

N- NO, IT'S NOTHING.

...?

I HEAR THAT YOU KILLED TWO VAMPANEZE.

PIKU (FLINCH)

THANKS.

IT'S NEARLY TIME FOR KURDA'S QUESTIONING TO BEGIN.

PASA (FLAP)

ARE YOU AWAKE, DARREN?

DID THEY BLIND YOUR OTHER EYE?!

RUINED. I'M BLIND AS A BAT NOW.

I AM, VANEZ. HOW IS THE EYE?

LARTEN? ARE YOU IN HERE?

IT'LL TAKE A WHILE TO GET USED TO, BUT I'LL ADAPT.

N! (GRIN)

IT'S NOT THE END OF THE WORLD, DARREN.

IT'S BETTER NOT TO FIGHT AT ALL.

NO, HARKAT...

BASHIN (SMACK)

I WISH I... COULD HAVE FOUGHT... WITH YOU!

COME, LET'S GO TO THE HALL OF PRINCES.

DARREN?

...YOU'D NEVER HAVE TO WORRY ABOUT KILLING OR BEING KILLED...

AT LEAST THAT WAY...

LOOKS LIKE THE PLACE IS PACKED.

ZAWA (MURMUR)

ZAWA (MURMUR)

IT'S DARREN SHAN!!

THE HERO HAS ARRIVED !!

COME, TO THE FRONT!

THE FLAVOUR... OF THE MOMENT.

FLAVOUR, HUH?

EVERYONE THINKS...IT WAS THANKS... TO YOU THAT... THE VAM- PANEZE...WERE DEFEATED.

FIRST- ROW SEATS?

OOO (OOOH)

UOOOO
(RAHHH)

BURU
(SHIVER)

BURU

HERE I AM, FACE-TO-FACE...

...WITH KURDA.

FOR THE INTERRO-GATION OF THE TRAITOR, KURDA SMAHLT!

ZAWA

WE KNOW WHY WE ARE HERE.

ZAWA

ORDER!

ZAWA
(MURMUR)

GOKU
(GULP)

JARA
(CLANK)

WERE YOU IN LEAGUE WITH THE VAM-PANEZE WE KILLED YESTER-DAY?

IS IT TRUE?

I WAS.

ANYONE WHO INTERRUPTS WILL BE THROWN OUT!!

I CALLED FOR ORDER!

WRETCH! KNOW SHAME!

TRAITOR!!

I WILL SPEAK THE TRUTH HERE. THE PLAN WAS MY OWN.

I KNOW WHAT YOU'LL DO, ARROW. I HAVE NO WISH TO BE TORTURED.

OR SO HELP ME, I'LL—

LIAR! TELL US WHO PUT YOU UP TO THIS!

MY OWN.

UPON WHOSE ORDERS WERE YOU ACTING?

I PROVIDED THEM WITH COPIES OF MY MAPS.

I ARRANGED FOR THE VAMPANEZE TO COME.

KURDA SMAHLT!!

YOU WILL PAY FOR YOUR CRIMES WITH DEATH!

LET ME KILL HIM!

RAAHH!!!

HIS DEATH WILL COME SOON ENOUGH. LET US HEAR HIM OUT.

PEACE, LARTEN. KURDA IS GOING NOWHERE.

MR. CREPS-LEY...

I COULD LEAP FORWARD NOW AND MAKE AN END OF HIM BEFORE ANYONE COULD STOP ME.

BECAUSE WE'D RUN OUT OF TIME! IT WAS NOW OR NEVER!

HAS NOBODY WONDERED WHY I CHOSE SUCH AN INOPPORTUNE MOMENT...

...TO INSTIGATE AN ATTACK?

YOU FIND THIS AMUSING?!

YOU REALLY DON'T UNDERSTAND...

HA HA HA...

NOW THAT IT HAS FAILED, I FEAR WE ARE DOOMED!!

OUR ONLY HOPE LAY IN AN IMMEDIATE, PREEMPTIVE STRIKE!!

NOT TO VANQUISH IT!!

AS I SAID, I MEANT TO SAVE OUR RACE!

THAT'S WHAT MAKES THIS SO PAINFUL.

SADLY, NO.

ARE YOU MAD?!

YOU ATTACKED WITH THE VAMPANEZE TO PREVENT AN ATTACK BY THE VAMPANEZE?!

WHAT'S THIS NONSENSE? WE HAD NO INTENTION OF ATTACKING THE VAMPANEZE!

WE SHOULD GO AHEAD AND...

THIS IS A WASTE OF TIME! HE'S PLAYING US FOR FOOLS.

IT WAS AN ATTACK BY THE VAMPANEZE.

IT WAS NOT ATTACK BY THE VAMPIRES I SOUGHT TO HALT.

MR. TINY HAS VISITED THE VAMPANEZE!

HAH...

シ...ン...
SHIIIN
(SILENCE)

KURDA, I HAVE BAD NEWS.

I HAD DEDICATED MYSELF TO THE TASK OF REUNITING THE VAMPIRES WITH THE VAMPANEZE.

HE CAME THREE YEARS AGO.

NEITHER GLALDA NOR I WISHED FOR WAR.

WE WORKED TOGETHER TO BRIDGE THE TWO SIDES.

...AND IS LEARNING THEIR WAYS.

BUT HE'S TAKEN HIS PLACE AMONG THEM...

HE IS STILL HUMAN—HE HASN'T BEEN BLOODED.

HE WAS DISCOVERED SIX MONTHS AGO.

...AND LEAD THEM AGAINST US! AND HE'LL WIN!!

HE'LL BE BLOODED, TAKE HIS PLACE AMONG THEM...

...I MIGHT HAVE BEEN ABLE TO WIN THEM OVER!

IF I'D GAINED CONTROL OF THE STONE OF BLOOD BEFORE HIS BLOODING...

MY ACT OF TREACHERY WAS THE LAST DESPERATE ROLL OF THE DICE!!

NOW THAT I'VE FAILED, THE WAY IS OPEN FOR HIM.

YOU'VE CLEARED THE WAY FOR MR. TINY'S PROPHECY TO COME TO PASS!

BA (SPIN)

CONGRATULATIONS, GENTLEMEN! AFTER TODAY'S GREAT VICTORY, NOTHING STANDS BETWEEN YOU AND A FUTILE WAR WITH THE VAMPANEZE!!

EVERY VAMPIRE IN THIS HALL IS DAMNED!

WHEN IT STOPS, OUR TIME IS FINISHED!

BAKIN (CRAKK)

AS OF TONIGHT, THE CLOCK IS TICKING!

IT IS YOUR LAST CHANCE TO BANG YOUR DRUMS AND BRAG ABOUT YOUR VALOUR!

ENJOY YOUR CELEBRATIONS!

EVEN IN DEATH, MAY YOU BE TRIUMPHANT !!!.

MAY YOU BE...

...TRIUM‐

THE VAMPANEZE LORD WILL BE BLOODED, TAKE HIS PLACE AMONG THEM, LEAD THEM AGAINST US, AND HE'LL WIN!

EVERY VAMPIRE IN THIS HALL—IN THIS WORLD—IS DAMNED!!!

OOO (AAAHH)

CHAPTER 53: JUDGEMENT

THEN HE OPENED HIS MOUTH ...

... GLITTERED IN THE CORNERS OF HIS SAD, BLUE EYES.

ANGRY, DESOLATE TEARS ...

AND THEN KURDA'S EYES FOUND MINE.

EVEN IN DEATH, MAY YOU BE TRIUMPHANT ...

...AND CROAKED SARCASTICALLY ...

CHAPTER 53:
JUDGEMENT

SHIIN
(SHHH)

THEN HOW DO YOU KNOW HE EXISTS?

NO, I WOULD HAVE KILLED HIM IF I HAD.

YOU HAVE SEEN THIS VAMPANEZE LORD?

AN-SWER HIM!!

I DON'T...

COFFIN OF...?

THE COFFIN OF FIRE.

...AROUND THE SAME TIME THAT HE GAVE US THIS MAGICAL DOME.

MR. TINY BESTOWED IT UPON THEM MANY CENTURIES AGO...

THE VAMPANEZE HAVE A UNIQUE COFFIN CALLED THE COFFIN OF FIRE.

IF ONE WHO IS DESTINED TO LEAD THE VAMPANEZE LIES WITHIN THE COFFIN, HE WILL EMERGE UNSCATHED. OTHERWISE, HE PERISHES IN THE FLAMES.

IT IS A TRIAL BY FIRE.

THE COFFIN HAS BEEN GUARDED BY A TROOP OF VAMPANEZE WHO CALL THEMSELVES THE CARRIERS OF DESTINY.

OOO (OOHH)

オオッ

BUT SIX MONTHS AGO...

...AND DIED.

OVER THE DECADES, MANY VAMPANEZE HAVE BRAVED THE COFFIN...

4

...A HUMAN LAY DOWN IN IT...

...FACED THE FLAMES, AND CAME OUT WHOLE.

IT IS HE WHO WILL BE THE LORD OF THE VAMPANEZE...

I...

......

...BETWEEN VAMPIRES AND VAMPANEZE.

I INTENDED TO FORCE A UNION...

...TO THE DEATH, IF REQUIRED.

...EVERY MEMBER OF THE CLAN WILL OBEY AND FOLLOW HIM...

ONCE HE HAS BEEN BLOODED...

DOYO

DOYO (MURMUR)

DOYO

THAT IS WHEN I DECIDED TO CHANCE A COUP.

...I KNEW IT WAS TOO LATE TO PUT IN PLACE A FAIR PEACE AGREEMENT.

WHEN I HEARD THAT THE VAMPANEZE LORD HAD BEEN UNEARTHED...

FOR ALL VAMPIRES TO ADOPT THE VAMPANEZE WAYS AND CUSTOMS.

IN SHORT, FOR US TO JOIN THE VAMPANEZE!

...OUR PEOPLE WOULD HAVE HAD NO CHOICE BUT TO AGREE TO MY TERMS.

IF I HAD HANDED THE STONE OF BLOOD TO THE VAMPANEZE...

AND WHAT WOULD THEY HAVE BEEN?

......

BUT IT'S PREFERABLE TO ANNIHILATION.

 I FIGURED YOU WOULD SAY THAT.

 IT'S AN OUTRAGE!

I'D RATHER DIE THAN DO ANY SUCH THING!

 KURDA...

GU... (CHRG)

EVEN IF YOU ALL HAD CHOSEN TO FIGHT TO THE DEATH, AT LEAST I'D HAVE TRIED.

 MANY AMONG THEM WISH TO AVOID A WAR, AS DO I.

THEY MADE NO OFFERS.

 WHAT WAS IN IT FOR YOU, KURDA? DID THE VAMPANEZE PROMISE YOU A TITLE? ONE GREATER THAN PRINCE?

 THEY HOPED TO PREVENT TOTAL, ALL-OUT CONFLICT...

...SPARING THEIR COLLEAGUES AND FRIENDS.

THAT'S WHY THIRTY-EIGHT AGREED TO ACCOMPANY ME ON THIS MISSION.

 ...LIKE VERMIN.

ZUKU (STAB)

THEY WERE VOLUNTEERS, BRAVE MEN WHOM YOU KILLED...

WHAT SACRIFICE?!

NOBLER THAN YOU IMAGINE!

HAVE YOU NO BRAINS? DON'T YOU SEE THE SACRIFICE I MADE?!

JARA (CLANK)

WE HAD NO ULTERIOR MOTIVES. WE DID IT FOR YOUR SAKES, NOT OUR OWN.

VERY NOBLE OF YOU, KURDA.

OH?

THE VAMPANEZE DESPISE TRAITORS EVEN MORE THAN WE DO!!

WIN OR LOSE, MY REWARD WOULD HAVE BEEN DEATH!

SFX: ZAWA (MURMUR) ZAWA

THE LAW IS WRITTEN INTO THE HEARTS OF EACH AND EVERY MEMBER OF THE CLANS.

NEITHER THE VAMPIRES NOR THE VAMPANEZE WILL SUFFER A TRAITOR TO LIVE.

GU (RRGH)

DOYO (MURMUR)

THEN, WHEN OUR PEOPLE'S FUTURE WAS ASSURED ...

...I'D HAVE OFFERED MYSELF UP TO THIS SEN- TENCE.

DOYO

...I'D HAVE REMAINED HERE TO OVERSEE THE MERGING OF OUR CLANS.

HAD EVERY- THING WORKED OUT...

I HAD ONLY THE BEST INTERESTS OF THE CLAN AT HEART.

THERE WAS NOTHING "IN IT" FOR ME.

IF ALL YOU HAVE SAID IS TRUE, WHY DID YOU NOT COME TO US?

I SOUGHT TO SAVE LIVES, NOT TAKE THEM.

THAT WAS NOT MY WISH.

BECAUSE YOUR SOLUTION WOULD HAVE BEEN TO KILL EVERY LIVING VAMPANEZE.

I HAVE FEW REGRETS ...

BUT IT DOESN'T CHANGE THE FACT ...

OH, KUR-DA...

... THAT YOU MURDERED GAVNER.

I TOOK A CHANCE, AND IT DIDN'T PAN OUT.

THAT'S LIFE.

BUT THE FUTURE OF OUR PEOPLE OUTWEIGHED ANY INDIVIDUAL.

IT WAS NOT MY WISH TO SHED BLOOD.

MY ONE REAL SOURCE OF SORROW WAS THAT I HAD TO KILL GAVNER PURL.

...IF IT MEANT SAFEGUARDING THE LIVES OF THE REST.

BU CCHOMP!

I'D HAVE KILLED A DOZEN MORE LIKE GAVNER IF I HAD TO. EVEN A HUNDRED...

SU (SHH)

WHY, KURDA ...?

BUT IF THAT WAS THE CASE, WHY SAVE ME?

EVEN AT THE RISK OF RUINING THE ENTIRE PLAN...

I AM TROUBLED BY WHAT YOU HAVE SAID.

I WOULD RATHER YOU HAD BEEN A NEFARIOUS TRAITOR, THAT I COULD SENTENCE YOU TO DEATH WITH CLEAR CONSCIENCE.

HAD I A CHOICE, I WOULD GRANT YOU THE RIGHT TO DIE ON YOUR FEET, AS A VAMPIRE, WITH PRIDE.

BUT AS A PRINCE, I HAVE NO CHOICE, ONLY A RESPONSIBILITY TO UPHOLD.

WHAT-EVER YOUR REASONS, YOU BETRAYED US...

...YOU MUST DIE.

...AND FOR THAT...

156

THE HALL OF DEATH.

...BUT WE MUST OBEY OUR CUSTOMS.

I DON'T KNOW IF IT'S JUST OR NOT...

HE SHOULD BE DISMEMBERED BEFORE CREMATION, SO THAT HIS SOUL MAY NEVER KNOW PARADISE.

I VOTE THAT HE BE TAKEN TO THE HALL OF DEATH AND SUMMARILY EXECUTED!

DOES ANYONE CARE TO SPEAK ON BEHALF OF THE TRAITOR?

GAKU
(SLUMP)

SOB...
SOB...

I DIDN'T LEARN THIS UNTIL LATER, WHEN SEBA TOLD ME.

ZAWA (MURMUR)

...WERE THE SIGN AMONG VAMPIRES FOR A TRAITOR OR ONE OF BAD STANDING.

THE THREE UGLY RED MARKS DRAWN ON KURDA'S CHEST...

NO ONE WILL... SPEAK ILL... OF HIM NOW.

KURDA WAS... A VERY STRONG MAN.

YOU... SHOULDN'T FEEL BAD.

I KNOW.

HE WAS TRUE... TO HIS VALUES.

NO...

YOU WON'T BE PRESENT AT... KURDA'S EXECUTION?

DO YOU HAVE ANY LAST WORDS?

...YOU WILL REMEMBER THE SACRIFICE THAT I MADE.

I WISH THAT IN THE LONG AND PAINFUL NIGHTS AHEAD ...

IT'S SAD..

I KNOW ...

AND THAT WAS THE END OF KURDA SMAHLT.

THE END OF A KILLER... A TRAITOR... MY FRIEND.

WHAT HAPPENS NOW, VANEZ? WILL YOU LEAVE VAMPIRE MOUNTAIN?

NO. ANY OTHER TIME...

...I'D HAVE STUMBLED AROUND IN THE OUTSIDE WORLD UNTIL I MET A NOBLE END, AS IS A BLIND VAMPIRE'S WAY.

CHAPTER 54: CEREMONY OF BLOOD

SEBA AND I WILL BE SUPPORTING OUR KIND FROM HERE!

I'M AFRAID MY RETIREMENT HAS BEEN PUT ON HOLD.

YOU TOO, SEBA?

I CAN STILL MAKE MYSELF USEFUL AROUND HERE.

BUT THE COMING OF THE VAMPANEZE LORD HAS CHANGED ALL OF THAT.

BUT THE ISSUE OF DARREN'S SENTENCING STILL REMAINS.

IT IS A MORE PRESSING CONCERN AT THIS TIME.

PERHAPS. MIKA HAS ALREADY ASKED ME ABOUT STAYING...

...AND PERHAPS RESUMING MY OFFICIAL GENERAL DUTIES.

DOES THAT MEAN THE QUARTER-MASTER JOB OFFER NO LONGER STANDS?

...BUT I AM SURE THE PRINCES WILL FIND SOME USE FOR YOU.

I AM AFRAID IT DOES.

I AM SURE HE WILL BE PARDONED.

NO. MIKA PROMISED TO REOPEN THE DEBATE AFTER THE FUNERAL CEREMONIES.

THE PRINCES HAVE NOT YET DETERMINED HIS FATE?

I PROMISED ARRA I WOULD NOT LET DARREN BE KILLED!

THEN ALTER THEM THEY SHALL!

THE PRINCES WOULD HAVE TO ALTER THE LAWS IN ORDER TO SPARE DARREN'S LIFE.

...THAT THE DEATH PENALTY HAS NEVER BEEN REVOKED.

I HOPE SO. BUT LARTEN, SURELY YOU KNOW...

HI, EVERY-ONE.

MR. CREPS-LEY.

...THAT HE HAD EARNED THE RIGHT TO LIFE.

SHE SAID, IN HER DYING BREATH...

NO, NOTHING.

IS SOME-THING WRONG?

OHON (AHEM)

OHO

GOHO

BU BU (KOFF)

GOHO (KOFF)

YEAH.

LET US ALL SEE GAVNER OFF NOW.

...FIND PARADISE...

HE DIED WITH HONOUR.

MAY HIS SPIRIT...

HIS NAME WAS GAVNER PURL.

KURDA TOLD THE GUARDS WHERE TO FIND THE HIDING PLACE FOR GAVNER'S BODY.

IT ALMOST LOOKS LIKE GAVNER IS SMILING.

KURDA ...

...TO KEEP IT FROM ROTTING AND ANIMALS.

ACCORDING TO THE SEARCH PARTY, IT WAS BURIED CAREFULLY UNDER THE SNOW...

VAMPIRES DON'T USUALLY ATTEND CREMATIONS IN SUCH NUMBERS. GAVNER WOULD BE HAPPY TO SEE IT.

THANKS FOR ALL YOU DID... TO SAVE MY LIFE.

HERE'S YOUR KNIFE BACK, GAVNER.

YES ...

...I KNOW ...

DO YOU WANT TO LEAVE?

SOB...

IT'S JUST ...

NO, I WANT TO STAY.

... HARD, YOU KNOW ?

...THE SMOKE RISING AND SLIPPING THROUGH THE CRACKS IN THE CEILING...

THERE WAS SOMETHING STRANGELY COMFORTING IN WATCHING THE FLAMES ENGULF GAVNER...

CHIRI
(ZZZK)

JIRI
(FFFF)

BOOO
(FWOOMM)

...WERE CREMATED, ONE BY ONE.

AFTER HIM, THE VAMPIRES WHO WERE KILLED IN THE BATTLE WITH THE VAMPANEZE...

BE BRAVE, LARTEN!

ARRA...

AND THEN IT WAS ARRA SAILS'S TURN TO BE CARRIED INTO THE CHAMBER.

I WILL CONDUCT MYSELF WITH ALL DUE DECORUM.

SHE WOULD NOT HAVE WANTED EMOTIONAL OUTBURSTS.

BUT...

...ALMOST AS IF IT WERE GAVNER'S SPIRIT DEPARTING.

...I MISS HER.

WITH ALL MY HEART AND SOUL, I MISS HER.

JUST AS HE'D SWORN HE WOULD BE...

...MR. CREPSLEY WAS ENTIRELY COMPOSED FOR THE LENGTH OF THE CREMATION.

...AND HIS CRIES ECHOED THROUGH THE CORRIDORS AND TUNNELS FAR INTO THE COLD, LONELY DAWN.

IT WAS ONLY LATER, WHEN HE WAS ALONE IN HIS CELL, THAT HE WEPT LOUDLY...

I HOPE THEY MADE IT BACK TO RUDI AND THE OTHERS SAFELY.

I NEVER HAD THE CHANCE TO SAY GOOD-BYE OR THANK THEM.

I SUPPOSE THEY SLIPPED AWAY TO REJOIN THEIR PACK.

I HAVEN'T SEEN STREAK OR THE OTHER WOLVES SINCE THAT DAY.

I KEPT A DIARY TO JOT DOWN MY STORY AS I WAITED ...

THE LONG WAIT BETWEEN THE CREMATIONS AND MY TRIAL WAS AWFUL.

BY THE TIME I WAS NEARLY DONE WRITING, MR. CREPSLEY AND SOME GUARDS CAME...

...TO INFORM ME OF THE UP-COMING TRIAL.

STILL, I WANTED TO GET EVERY-THING STRAIGHT INSIDE MY HEAD.

...BUT IT FILLED ME WITH THE EERIE SENSATION THAT I WAS WRITING MY OWN WILL.

...IF THINGS MIGHT NOT HAVE ENDED A BETTER WAY FOR KURDA.

IN PARTICU-LAR, I COULDN'T HELP BUT WONDER ...

PLEASE.

...I WANT YOU TO HAVE THIS DIARY.

IF THEY DECIDE TO EXECUTE ME...

ALL RIGHT ...

......

ME TOO. I WON'T LET...THEM DO ANYTHING... CRAZY TO YOU.

BASHI (FWAP)

BE BRAVE. IF ANYTHING HAPPENS, I SHALL COME TO YOUR AID.

DARREN!

RGH...

YEAH, JUST A LITTLE NERVOUS.

ARE YOU OKAY?

ZA (BOW)

VERY WELL.

AS YOU PLEASE.

NO. WE WILL REMAIN.

THIS IS DARREN'S TRIAL.

LARTEN, LITTLE PERSON, YOU MAY STEP DOWN NOW.

... AND WE HAD NO CHOICE BUT TO EXECUTE HIM.

BUT NOW, ONE OF OUR KIND HAS BETRAYED US, EVEN IF IT WAS FOR THE SAKE OF OUR OWN GOOD...

FOR CENTURIES, WE VAMPIRES HAVE STUCK BY OUR OLD WAYS AND TRADITIONS, SPARING NO THOUGHT FOR NEW IDEAS.

THESE ARE STRANGE TIMES.

...DEATH!!!

THIS CRIME IS PUNISHABLE IN ONLY ONE WAY...

...AND THEN FLED FROM HIS SENTENCING.

DARREN FAILED THE TRIALS OF INITIATION...

SOME HAVE ARGUED FOR PERMANENT CHANGES TO THE LAW THAT WOULD GRANT DARREN FREEDOM ...

AFTER THIS BETRAYAL, WE MUST NOW OPEN OUR EYES, EARS, AND HEARTS TO NEW WAYS OF THINKING AND LIVING.

OH!!

DARREN HAS ENDURED GREAT PAIN AND SACRIFICED HIS FREEDOM FOR THE GOOD OF THE CLAN. HE HAS FOUGHT BRAVELY AND PROVEN HIS WORTH.

BUT TIMES HAVE CHANGED.

...BUT AFTER LENGTHY DEBATE, WE HAVE DECIDED AGAINST ALTERING OUR LAWS.

CHARNA'S GUTS! I WILL NOT STAND FOR THIS!!

BA CLEAP?

I'LL BE PUT TO DEATH.

SO IT'S TRUE.

SFX: BURU (SHIVER)

MR. CREPS-LEY! HAR-KAT!

THE SAME GOES... FOR ME...

ANYONE WISHING TO LAY HANDS ON MY ASSISTANT WILL FIRST HAVE TO LAY HIS HANDS ON ME!

DARREN RISKED HIS LIFE FOR YOU, AND NOW YOU WOULD SENTENCE HIM TO DEATH? NEVER!

STAND QUIETLY AND LISTEN TO YOU SENTENCE DARREN TO DEATH? I THINK NOT!

HEAR PARIS OUT UNTIL THE FINISH.

SELF-CONTROL, LARTEN.

I DO NOT UNDERSTAND. HOW CAN DARREN BE SAVED WITHOUT CHANGING THE LAW?!

AN... HONOURABLE WAY?

IT SUDDENLY SURFACED IN THE OCEAN OF MY BRAIN, LIKE A FISH.

I DON'T KNOW HOW I THOUGHT OF IT.

ARROW WAS THE FIRST TO SUGGEST AN HONOURABLE WAY OUT OF THE DILEMMA.

WHO AMONG US ARE IMMUNE TO PUNISHMENT? WHO COULD FAIL THE TRIALS AND WALK AWAY UNTOUCHED?

USE YOUR HEAD, LARTEN.

WE NEED NOT BEND OR CHANGE LAWS TO SUIT DARREN'S PURPOSES. WE NEED ONLY PLACE HIM ABOVE THEM.

HE'S EARNED THE RIGHT TO BEAR THE TITLE. MORE THAN ANY OF US HERE, PERHAPS, HE IS WORTHY.

THAT DOES NOT MATTER! WE'RE NOT INTERESTED IN THE FINE PRINT.

BA (WHOOSH)

MR. CREPSLEY?

WHAT ARE THEY SAYING?

YOU CANNOT MEAN...?

HE IS NOT A GENERAL! HE IS NOT EVEN A FULL VAMPIRE!

HA HA...

HE IS TOO YOUNG!

ABOVE THE LAW...?

HA (GASP)

I RAN OVER MY FIRST INTRODUCTION OVER AND OVER IN MY HEAD. IT WOULDN'T DO TO LEAVE A BAD FIRST IMPRESSION.

DARREN-SAN WAS ALREADY IN THE MEETING ROOM.

...AND THEN IT WAS SHOWTIME.

I HAD A QUICK MEETING ABOUT WHAT TO SAY TO DARREN-SAN BEFORE I MET HIM...

Too nervous to remember any of it.

DAKU (DRIP)

ダク

ダク DAKU

E- EXCUSE...

GACHA (CLICK)

AND THEN...

PEKAA (FLAAASH)

THE AURA DARREN-SAN PROJECTED WAS SO POWERFUL, I WAS INSTANTLY PUSHED ABOUT 2.3 INCHES BACKWARD.

ZURIRI (ZWOOOP)

...MEEEEEE!!!...

...UNTIL I REALIZED, WITH A HORRIBLE START...

OH!!!...

DID I DO SOMETHING RUDE? WAS MY PRONUNCIATION SO BAD THAT HE COULDN'T UNDERSTAND ME? THE AWKWARD MOMENT STRETCHED ON AND ON...

GASHI (GRAB)

FACE-TO-FACE WITH AN INTERNATIONALLY BEST-SELLING AUTHOR, I TUMBLED THROUGH MY PANICKED OPENING STATEMENTS.

DARREN-SAN LOOKED SLIGHTLY TROUBLED...

OH NO!

I NEVER INTRODUCED MYSELF!!!

FROM THIS POINT ON, WE HELD A VERY CALM AND ENJOYABLE INTERVIEW.

He was born to hold a wine glass!

IN A WORD, HE WAS A GENTLEMAN!

DARREN-SAN WAS TRULY COURTEOUS AND REFINED IN PERSON.

NO DOUBT POOR DARREN-SAN THOUGHT HE WAS BEING ACCOSTED BY SOME OBSESSED ASIAN FAN...

OHHH! ARAI!!

M-MY NAME IS...

PON (PAT)

PON

PON

HE WAS GENTLE AND KIND, AND HIS BOYISH EYES LEFT A STRONG IMPRESSION ON ME.

° WOW...

BUT IT WAS WHEN WE DISCUSSED HIS STORY-MAKING POLICIES AND HABITS THAT I WAS TRULY AMAZED. FOR BEING A MAN WITH SUCH SPECIFIC DETAILS AND DESIRES, HE WAS VERY FORGIVING AND EASYGOING WITH THE PROCESS OF PRODUCING A MANGA EDITION.

I DIDN'T SEE HIM EAT MANY VEGETABLES THAT NIGHT.

He used chopsticks with the stew and ate it with raw egg.

I FOUND OUT THAT DARREN-SAN'S FAVOURITE IS "MEAT"!!

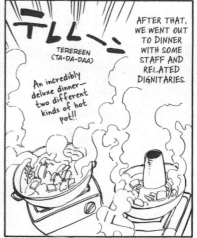

TEREREEN (TA-DA-DAA)

An incredibly deluxe dinner—two different kinds of hot pot!!

AFTER THAT, WE WENT OUT TO DINNER WITH SOME STAFF AND RELATED DIGNITARIES.

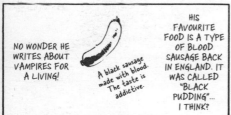

NO WONDER HE WRITES ABOUT VAMPIRES FOR A LIVING!

A black sausage made with blood. The taste is addictive.

HIS FAVOURITE FOOD IS A TYPE OF BLOOD SAUSAGE BACK IN ENGLAND. IT WAS CALLED "BLACK PUDDING"... I THINK?

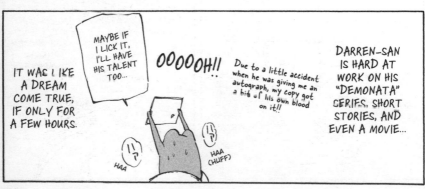

IT WAS LIKE A DREAM COME TRUE, IF ONLY FOR A FEW HOURS.

MAYBE IF I LICK IT, I'LL HAVE HIS TALENT TOO...

OOOOOH!!

Due to a little accident when he was giving me an autograph, my copy got a bit of his own blood on it!!

HAA

HAA (HUFF)

DARREN-SAN IS HARD AT WORK ON HIS "DEMONATA" SERIES, SHORT STORIES, AND EVEN A MOVIE...

HOWEVER, ALL MY FRIENDS AND FAMILY WHO SAW THE PHOTO OF ME THAT RAN WITH THE INTERVIEW SAID, "YOU LOOK OLDER," OR, "YOU SHOULD EAT A BIT HEALTHIER, LAY OFF ALL THAT MEAT." NOT SURE HOW I FEEL ABOUT THAT.

NOT ONLY THAT, BUT THE TEXT OF OUR INTERVIEW WAS PRINTED ON DELUXE COLOUR PAGES IN THE PAGES OF WEEKLY SHONEN SUNDAY TWO MONTHS LATER!

GOHHH
(ZWOOOM)

SEE YOU AGAIN!

I'M SURE THAT SOME OF YOU READING THIS MANGA WERE PRESENT AT THE SIGNING TOO.

DARREN-SAN HAD ANOTHER AUTOGRAPH SIGNING THE NEXT DAY.

......

PON (PAT)

PON

THANK YOU ALL SO MUCH!!!

I WOULD LIKE TO THANK DARREN-SAN, THE FOLKS FROM THE EDITORIAL DEPARTMENT, OTHER DIGNITARIES, AND ALL OF THE READERS FOR MAKING THIS HAPPEN.

HEH HEH HEH...

WHAT HAPPENS NOW, MR. CREPSLEY?

NOW THAT DARREN HAS SHOCKINGLY BEEN PROMOTED TO VAMPIRE PRINCE, WHAT MIGHT FATE HAVE IN STORE FOR HIM?

I'LL SEE YOU AGAIN IN VOLUME 7!!

WHILE I FEEL ENORMOUS GRATITUDE AT WHAT I'VE ACCOMPLISHED SO FAR, I ALSO FEEL SAD THAT THERE'S ONLY HALF LEFT TO TELL.

SO, AT THIS POINT, THE MANGA EDITION HAS COVERED PRECISELY HALF OF THE ORIGINAL STORY.

The End

THE SAGA OF DARREN SHAN ⑥
The Vampire Prince

Darren Shan
Takahiro Arai

Translation: Stephen Paul
Lettering: AndWorld Design
Art direction: Hitoshi SHIRAYAMA
Original cover design: Shigeru ANZAI + Bay Bridge Studio

Darren Shan Vol. 6
Text © 2007 Darren Shan, Artworks © 2007 Takahiro ARAI
All rights reserved
Original Japanese edition published in Japan in 2007
by Shogakukan Inc., Tokyo
Artwork reproduction rights in U.K. and The Commonwealth arranged
with Shogakukan Inc. through Tuttle-Mori Agency, Inc., Tokyo.

English translation © Darren Shan 2010

Published in Great Britain by Harper Collins *Children's Books* 2010
Harper Collins *Children's Books* is a division of HarperCollins *Publishers* Ltd
77-85 Fulham Palace Road, Hammersmith, London, W6 8JB

www.harpercollins.co.uk

ISBN: 978 0 00 733273 1

Printed and bound in Great Britain by Clays Ltd, St Ives plc

Mixed Sources
Product group from well-managed
forests and other controlled sources
www.fsc.org Cert no. SW-COC-1806
© 1996 Forest Stewardship Council

FSC is a non-profit international organisation established to promote the
responsible management of the world's forests. Products carrying the FSC
label are independently certified to assure consumers that they come
from forests that are managed to meet the social, economic and
ecological needs of present and future generations.

Find out more about HarperCollins and the environment at
www.harpercollins.co.uk/green